GARFIELD'S
TALES OF
MYSTERY

Created by
JIM DAVIS
Written by Jim Kraft
Illustrated by Mike Fentz

PAWS, INC.

Publishers · GROSSET & DUNLAP · *New York*

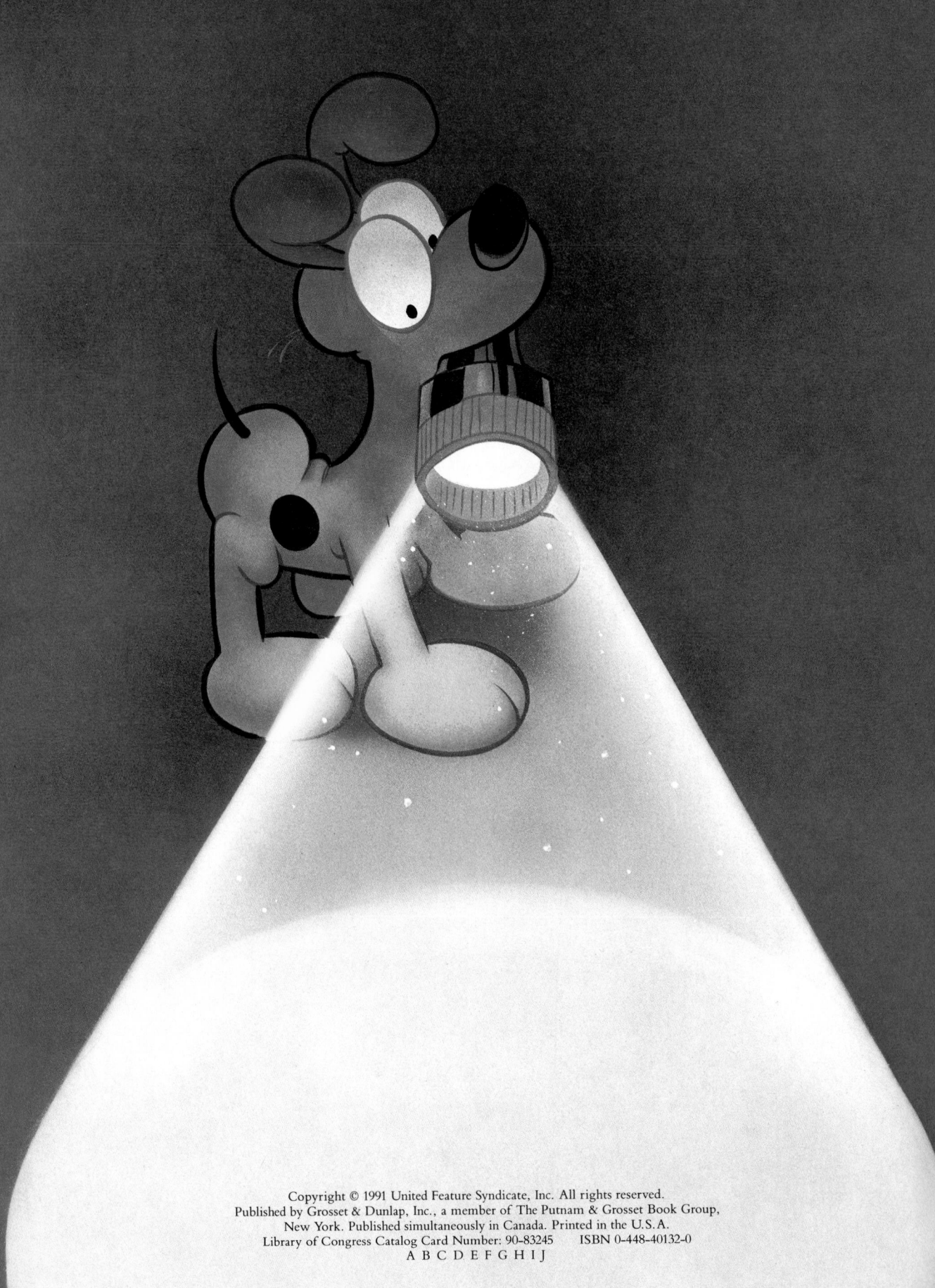

Contents

The Clue
in the Chicken Coop

"It's the chickens!" Mrs. Arbuckle said to Jon over the phone. "Come quick!"

Jon, Garfield, and Odie raced off to the Arbuckle farm.

"Every morning I find another hen," said Mrs. Arbuckle. "You remember that we've always kept ten. Never more, because your father can't stand them. Says they're messy and not real bright."

"But they look great on a plate," remarked Garfield.

"And then, out of the blue, on Tuesday I counted eleven. Wednesday there were twelve. Every morning another one. This morning it was fifteen. And I don't know where they're coming from. Of course, I can't tell your father; he'd have a fit. And your brother, Doc Boy, is no help. He's too busy with his girlfriend."

"Doc Boy has a girlfriend?" asked Jon.

"I thought he was going steady with the tractor," said Garfield.

"Anna Mae Fleener," replied Mrs. Arbuckle. "Her dad used to have the egg business. Doc Boy's been out late every night this week."

"Have you noticed anything else unusual?" Jon asked.

"Well, one of my aprons is missing."

"Don't worry, Mom. I'll get to the bottom of this," said Jon.

"Right after lunch," added Garfield.

After lunch, Garfield and Odie checked out the chicken coop. While Odie nosed around for clues, Garfield questioned the new hens, with no success.

"Those dumb clucks are no help," he told Odie. "All they know is they crossed a road. But they can't figure out why. You find anything?"

Odie sniffed the air, then wrinkled his nose.

Garfield sniffed. "Something's rotten in this chicken coop," he said.

Next, the pet detectives inspected the farmhouse. They checked Mr. and Mrs. Arbuckle's room. Then Garfield spent a long time investigating the refrigerator. After that, they peeked into Doc Boy's room.

Doc Boy's good overalls were laid out on the bed. Must have another date tonight, thought Garfield.

Once again, Odie sniffed the air and wrinkled his nose. He pointed to a bottle on Doc Boy's dresser.

" 'Old Socks' after-shave," said Garfield. "This certainly smells—ugh!—familiar. Hmm. Doc Boy's had a date every night this week. Odie, we're on to something. Let's find Jon."

Jon was in the barn, gluing feathers to some feed sacks. "I'm making a chicken disguise," he told his pets.

"Jon, we're not interested in your weird hobbies," said Garfield.

"Tonight I'll put this on and hide in the coop. If someone sneaks in with a chicken, I'll nab him." He pulled on the costume. "Well? How do I look?"

"Like a big turkey," said Garfield. "But what else is new?"

That night Jon, Garfield, and Odie waited in the darkened chicken coop.

"I'm glad you boys are here," said Jon. "I was going to ask Doc Boy to join me, but he had a date. Why don't I ever have a date?"

"Most women aren't attracted to poultry," observed Garfield.

At that moment, they heard footsteps approaching the chicken coop. The hinges squeaked softly as the door opened. A shadowy figure stepped into the coop.

"Gotcha!" cried Jon, turning on his flashlight. There stood a startled, apron-clad Doc Boy, holding an equally startled chicken!

"Doc Boy?" said Jon.

"Unhand that hen!" cried Garfield.

Blinded by the light, Doc Boy stepped into a bucket of seed and crashed into a row of sleeping hens, who began a frightful squawking.

"What's going on in there?" called Jon's father. Mr. and Mrs. Arbuckle peered into the chicken coop. They saw Doc Boy in Mrs. Arbuckle's apron and Jon in his chicken suit. "I love you boys," said Mr. Arbuckle, "but you got a strange idea of fun."

Once the feathers stopped flying, Doc Boy confessed everything. "I did it for Anna Mae. Her father was going to sell the chickens, and she couldn't bear to see them all go. So I bought some of them. Thought if I snuck them into the chicken coop one at a time, no one would notice."

"How many were you going to sneak in?" asked Mrs. Arbuckle.

"Fifty."

"Trust me. They'd have noticed," said Garfield.

"I never would have suspected *you*, Doc Boy," said Mrs. Arbuckle.

"I did," said Garfield. "I had a hunch the missing apron was a clue. Why would someone steal an apron? To protect their clothes. And who around here had been wearing his good clothes? Doc Boy. When Odie and I smelled that 'Old Socks' after-shave in the chicken coop *and* in Doc Boy's room, I knew we had our man. But we had to catch him in the act."

"Thank goodness this is all over," said Mrs. Arbuckle. "Let's celebrate with a midnight snack. I'll bet you could eat something, right, Garfield?"

Garfield grinned. "That's no mystery!"

The Purloined Pie

Garfield and Odie watched as Jon took a cherry pie from the oven and quickly slipped it into an empty bird cage. Then Jon threw off his oven mitts, slammed the door of the cage, and padlocked it.

"Do you know what this is, Garfield?" asked Jon, holding up the cage.

"A pie in a bird cage," said Garfield. "Good luck teaching it to sing."

Jon hung the cage from a hook in the kitchen ceiling. "It's my foolproof way of keeping your paws off this pie I baked for the party tonight at Grandma's. The cage is locked and I have the only key. And, as an added precaution, I've moved all the chairs into the dining room and locked the door. So don't think you can stack them up to reach the cage."

"He doesn't trust me, Odie," said Garfield. "I respect that."

Jon peered out the window. "It's stopped snowing," he said, putting on his coat. "So I'm off to the barbershop. Good-bye, Garfield. I hope the smell of that pie doesn't make you too hungry."

"Oh, go get a haircut," said Garfield.

An hour later Jon returned. He immediately checked the cage. The lock was unlocked. The door was open. The pie was gone!

"But how?!" cried Jon. "It's impossible! Garfield!"

Garfield sauntered into the kitchen, with Odie bouncing along

behind him. "Whatever it is, Odie did it," said Garfield.

"Garfield, you stole my pie!"

"I never touched a crumb."

"I know you did, Garfield," said Jon. "And I'll prove it."

First Jon examined Garfield's paws. "Evidence!" he exclaimed. "Look at this blue thread stuck to your claws. It's the same color blue as my oven mitts!"

"Jon," cried Garfield, "when did you finally learn your colors?"

Jon also checked Odie's paws, which were cold and wet. "Hmm," he said. "You've been outside." Jon studied the floor. "I see streaks leading toward the door. Streaks where you tried to wipe away the tracks." He marched to the trash can. "Tried to wipe them away with *this!*" Jon held up a ball of wet and dirty paper towels.

Finally Jon noticed a screwdriver on the counter. He picked it up. "The last piece of the puzzle," he said.

"Use it to tighten your brain," snapped Garfield.

Jon thought for a moment. Then he smiled with satisfaction. "Solving this mystery was incredibly simple for a mind like mine."

"Simple solutions for simple minds," said Garfield.

"Garfield, you needed a way to reach the cage. But the chairs were all locked away. So you had Odie build a big snowball in the yard and roll it into the kitchen. That's why his paws are cold. Then Odie stood on the snowball and *you* stood on Odie. You used the screwdriver to open the lock. But the pie was still hot. You had to grab it with oven mitts, and that left a telltale thread in your claws. After that, Odie rolled the snowball back out the door, and you used the towels to wipe up the melted snow. There, I've solved the mystery."

"Nice try, Jon," said Garfield, "but you couldn't solve your way out of a paper bag."

At that moment the phone rang. It was Jon's grandmother.

"Grandma, I have some bad news about your pie," said Jon.

"Really?" said Grandma. "Why, it looks fine to me."

"*You* have the pie?" said Jon.

"Of course. I stopped by while you were gone. By the way, Odie was scratching at the door, so I let him out. Naturally he tracked snow all over the kitchen when he came back in. But I wiped it up with paper towels."

"Ohhh," said Jon.

"Why was the pie in a cage? Had a tough time opening that lock with my hairpin. Fortunately, I haven't completely lost the knack!"

"But the screwdriver—" said Jon.

"That's the one I borrowed from you last month. Thought you might want it back. Try the cookies I left. See you at the party."

Jon hung up the phone and slumped to the floor. "The paper towels, the screwdriver, the culprits; I had it all wrong, Garfield."

"Well, Jon, it won't be the last time."

"But what about that thread in your claws?"

"Remember the blue drapes in the living room? While you were out, they met with an untimely shredding."

Jon sighed. "Guess I'm not such a great detective."

"That's elementary, my dear Arbuckle."

Jon stood up. An empty plate on the counter caught his eye.

"Hey!" said Jon. "What happened to the cookies Grandma left me?"

Garfield patted his tummy. "Gee, Jon. I haven't a clue."

The Secret of the Slippery Hippo

"It's nice of you to give Garfield and me a tour of the museum, Mr. Nash," Jon said to the assistant curator of the Natural History Museum.

"I saw you fumbling with your map and thought you might need help," Mr. Nash replied. "Besides, I love showing off our collection, especially our Egyptian artifacts. Are you interested in Egyptology?"

"Egypt-what?" asked Jon.

"Egyptology. That's the study of ancient Egypt. Very interesting people, the ancient Egyptians. Did you know they worshipped cats?"

"Doesn't everyone?" asked Garfield.

"They built the pyramids, of course. And they wrote with these pictures, called hieroglyphics." Mr. Nash showed them a stone tablet engraved with rows of tiny pictures.

"Here's my favorite piece in the collection," said Mr. Nash, pointing to a small blue hippopotamus. "It's almost four thousand years old." Mr. Nash removed the hippo from its glass case. "Would you like to hold it?"

"Oh, I couldn't," said Jon.

"We don't let everyone do it," whispered Mr. Nash. "But you seem so interested."

Jon reached cautiously for the figurine. Then suddenly the hippo was in the air. Jon dove for it, but the hippo slipped through his fingers and smashed to pieces on the floor!

"What have you done?" Mr. Nash screamed. "Guard! Guard!"

"It wasn't my fault!" exclaimed Jon.

"I hope that hippo had a four-thousand-year warranty," Garfield said.

A guard ran up to Mr. Nash.

"This man tried to steal a priceless antique," said Mr. Nash. "Take him to the curator's office. Follow me."

"What? It's a mistake!" Jon protested, as the guard marched him away.

"How's the food in prison?" Garfield asked the guard.

Mr. Stimson, head curator of the museum, was seated behind his desk. Angrily Mr. Nash told him about the broken hippo.

"Arbuckle," said Mr. Stimson, "that piece you tried to steal was going to a very important museum show in New York City. Now it's ruined. And you're in big trouble."

"But . . . but . . . ," stammered Jon.

"Gentlemen," Garfield said, "my client pleads 'not guilty' by reason of stupidity."

"But I wasn't stealing it!" Jon blurted out. "Mr. Nash asked if I wanted to hold it!"

"Nonsense!" snapped Mr. Nash. "I was getting the hippo ready for the exhibit when you snatched it away."

"I object!" interrupted Garfield. "The witness is fibbing!"

"And look at the hippo now," continued Mr. Nash, holding up a plastic bag filled with broken pieces.

"I'm calling the police," said Mr. Stimson.

"Hold on!" said Garfield. He leaped onto the desk and snatched the bag of pottery pieces away from Mr. Nash.

"Hey!" shouted Mr. Nash. "Give that back!"

Garfield dumped the pottery pieces onto Mr. Stimson's desk. "It's really just a *little* destroyed," said Garfield. Frantically he began trying to put the hippo back together.

"What's going on here?" demanded Mr. Stimson.

Garfield quickly fit together two pieces with designs on them.

"See? This will be good as new," Garfield said. "You can even read the hieroglyphics."

He added another piece. "Personally, I think these cracks give it more character," he said. Suddenly Garfield froze. He stared at the fragments in his paw.

"Jon, you're saved!" cried Garfield. "If this hippo is priceless, then I'm a mummy's uncle!"

Mr. Stimson examined the pieces Garfield held out to him. "Nash, is this the hippo that Mr. Arbuckle dropped?"

"Of course."

"But this hippo is a fake!"

"Impossible!" snapped Mr. Nash.

"It's true," said Garfield. "Look. These designs aren't hieroglyphics, they're letters."

Jon looked closely at the fragments. "When you put them together, they spell 'Taiwan.' What does that mean?"

"It means this hippo was made in Taiwan, not ancient Egypt," said Mr. Stimson. "This is a copy from the museum gift shop."

"Someone must have switched it for the original," Mr. Nash suggested.

"Obviously," said Mr. Stimson. "Why didn't you notice that?"

"Well, I . . . ," Mr. Nash began.

"You took the hippo out of its case," interrupted Mr. Stimson. "You must have seen that it was a fake. Explain yourself, Nash."

Mr. Nash started for the door. "Not so fast!" yelled Garfield. He dove onto Mr. Nash's back, sending him sprawling.

Mr. Nash groaned. "I give up. I dropped the original hippo yesterday. Then I panicked and replaced it with a fake. But I knew the switch would be discovered at the museum show. So I decided to trick someone into breaking the fake. Then no one would suspect me. I chose Mr. Arbuckle because he looked so clumsy."

"Not to mention gullible," said Garfield.

Mr. Nash was led away by the guard. Mr. Stimson apologized to Jon for all the trouble. "It's lucky for you your cat spotted that fake," he told Jon.

"Well, it's not easy to trick Garfield," said Jon.

"Like they say, Jon," observed Garfield, "you can fool some of the *people* all of the time . . . but don't ever try to con a cat!"

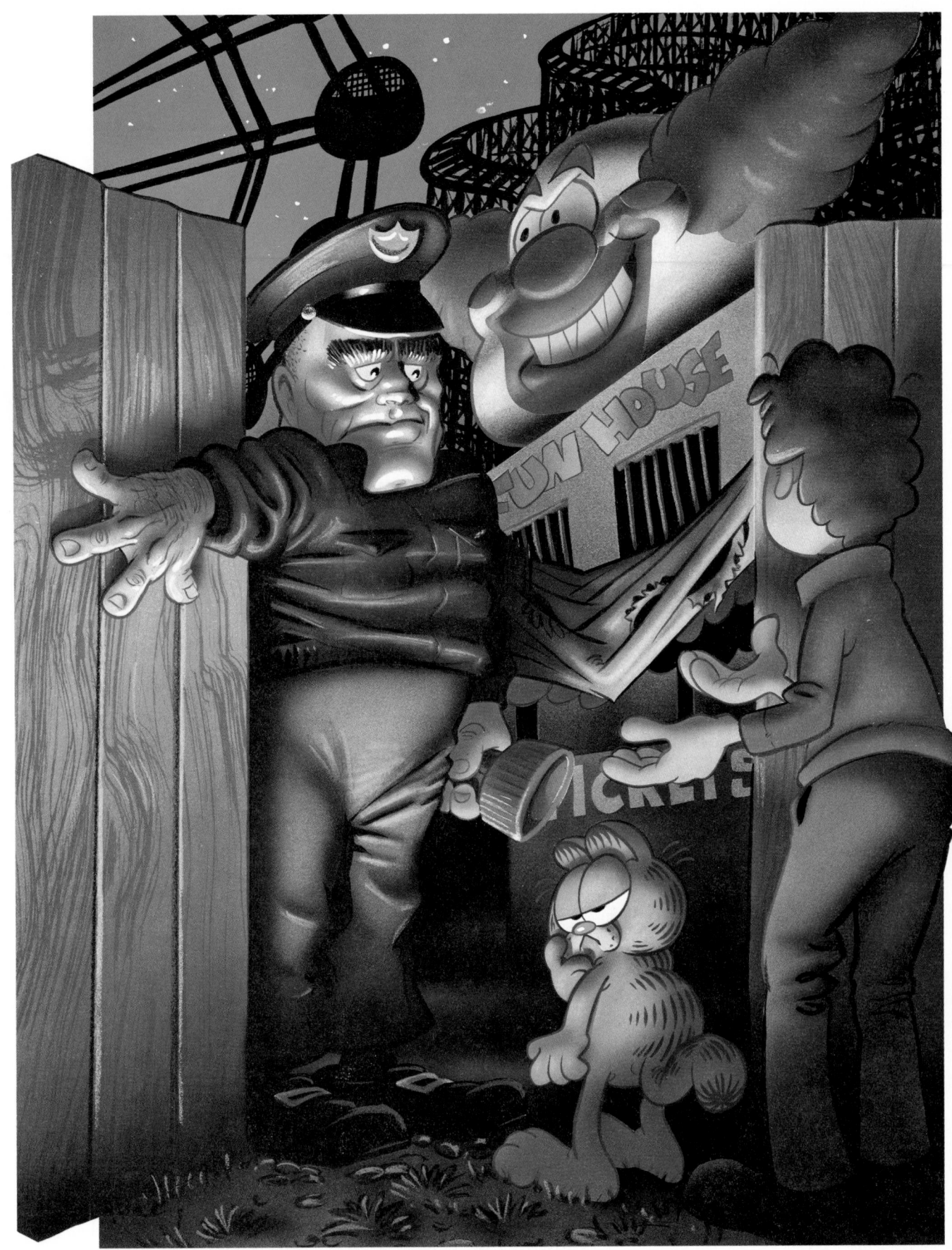

The Phantom of Funland

The old amusement park had been closed for years, and the wooden gate creaked as the grim night watchman opened it. Jon and Garfield stepped inside.

"What do you want?" asked the watchman.

"We're looking for my dog," Jon explained. "Odie was chasing fireflies and followed them through a hole in your fence. He does stuff like that."

"Because he has more tongue than brains," muttered Garfield. He glanced at the decaying buildings. "This place is creepy. Let's find Odie and get out."

"I've heard Funland is haunted," Jon said to the watchman. "Is it true?"

"Beware of the Phantom," was all the watchman said.

"The Phantom?" cried Garfield. "On second thought, Odie can find his own way home. Let's go, Jon. We're missing 'Fun with Fungus' on public television."

Jon gulped. "Is there really a Phantom?"

"Beware," the watchman repeated. Then he vanished into the night.

"I hear my teddy bear calling," said Garfield, turning to leave.

"Hold it, Garfield!" said Jon. "We can't leave Odie here."

"Oh, all right," Garfield grumbled. "But I really hate being haunted."

Jon and Garfield began searching the park. They crept past the old fun house, where a giant, plaster clown's head grinned eerily on the moonlit roof. They peeked into the dark arcade. They checked the shadows under the roller coaster. But there was no Odie.

As they passed the fun house again, a maniacal scream echoed down the midway. Jon and Garfield froze in their tracks. Then a shadow on the fun house roof caught Garfield's eye. "Jon, I see some—" But Garfield couldn't finish. The giant clown's head was hurtling toward them!

"Look out!" cried Garfield, pushing Jon aside. The clown's head smashed onto the ground, barely missing them.

"Jon, someone really doesn't want us here," said Garfield. "I mean, someone besides me!"

Trembling at every shadow, they continued to search. But Odie was nowhere to be found. Finally they sat down on the darkened carousel.

Suddenly the carousel lit up and started spinning!

"Whoa!" cried Jon, as he and Garfield scrambled onto horses.
"Who started this thing?"

"I did," said a low, sinister voice.

Slowly Jon and Garfield turned around. Riding behind them was
. . . the Phantom! His bony fingers reached for Garfield while with
his other, black-gloved hand he held tightly to the lurching horse.

"Nice ride," said Garfield. "Well, we have to panic now. See ya!"

With a shriek Jon and Garfield leaped off the carousel and raced
away. The Phantom chased after them.

Desperate to escape, Garfield veered through the door of the fun house. Immediately the floor dropped away, and he tumbled down a long slide into the darkness. He finally skidded to a halt at the bottom . . . only to come face-to-face with another gruesome creature! Garfield screamed. The creature screamed. Then the creature gave Garfield a familiar, sloppy lick.

"Odie!" said Garfield, hugging his friend. "You goofy mutt! Thanks to you, we're all going to be Phantom fodder! We've got to find Jon and get out of here!"

First they had to find a way out of the fun house. Garfield spied a strip of light. "Must be a door," he said. He eased it open.

The room was bare except for a cot and a pile of clothes.

"Look! Here's the watchman's uniform," Garfield said. "But where's the watchman?"

Odie stuck his nose under the cot and came out with a black glove. Garfield examined it closely. "Odie, I'm beginning to think that Phantom is a phony. Let's find out!"

When the two pets finally found their way out of the fun house, they heard Jon crying, "Help! Help!" They dashed toward the sound.

The Phantom had cornered Jon beneath the Ferris wheel.

"Drop that Arbuckle!" cried Garfield. Rushing forward, he threw himself on the control lever. The Ferris wheel started to spin, scooping the Phantom into a seat!

Garfield spun the Ferris wheel back and forth very fast. After a few minutes the Phantom cried, "I give up! I give up! Make it stop!"

When the Phantom reached the bottom, Garfield hit the brake. The Phantom lurched forward. "I don't feel so good," he moaned, slowly removing his mask.

"The night watchman!" exclaimed Jon.

"I believe this is yours," said Garfield, handing the watchman a black glove.

"Why were you scaring us?" Jon demanded.

"To keep you from snooping around here," explained the man, who was still a little pale. "My name is Higgins. I used to be the night watchman at Funland. When the park closed, I stayed behind."

"Why would you hang around this creepy place?" asked Jon.

"I love this old park," Higgins said. "It's been my home for thirty years. But I knew if the owners found out I was here, they'd make me leave. So I created the Phantom to scare nosy people away. Now I'll have to go," he said sadly.

"Mr. Higgins, I'll keep your secret," said Jon. "But on one condition: you have to let me visit you. I want to ride that carousel again!"

"It's a deal," said Mr. Higgins with a smile.

"I'll come back, too," added Garfield. "But you have to promise me *two* things: no ghosts and tons of cotton candy!"

The Case of
the All-Gone Goldfish

Inspector Garfield paced back and forth, ignoring the suspect slumped in the chair a few feet away.

"I need answers," said Garfield. "I need facts. And above all, I need oxygen. This pacing is too much exercise!

"Okay, here's the way I see it," said Garfield, after a rest. "A dull but appetizing goldfish named Bubbles disappears from Jon's fish tank. Bubbles's exact whereabouts are unknown, but it's a good bet she's gone to that big seafood platter in the sky, right?"

The suspect said nothing.

"Numerous paw prints are found on and around the fish tank," continued Garfield. "Paw prints which could very well be yours." He shot a quick glance at the suspect, checking his reaction. The suspect returned a cold, unblinking stare.

"You're tough, huh?" asked Garfield. "Well, I'm tough, too. I've touched Jon's dirty socks and survived. Believe me, it will go easier for you if you cooperate."

No response.

"All right then, have it your way," snapped Garfield. He resumed his explanation of the case. "You spent the day in the house with Bubbles. So you had plenty of opportunity. Plus, you had a motive. First of all, your kind has a taste for fish. To you Bubbles didn't belong in a fish tank; she belonged on a sesame-seed bun. With

maybe some onion rings on the side. And cheesecake for dessert!" Garfield licked his lips and checked his pockets, hoping he might find a pizza. But no luck.

"Uh, where was I? Oh, yes. But there was another motive: jealousy. You were jealous of the attention Bubbles received. Jealous of the fact that she had her own little castle to sleep in, while you had to share a bed. So you did it. You lured her out of the castle. Then you hit her with the tartar sauce!"

The suspect remained mute.

Garfield pursed his lips. "Still won't confess, eh?" He reached for a large paper bag and stood before the suspect, hands behind his back. "Okay," said Garfield. "Maybe you'll talk now!" Garfield pulled a little scuba mask and snorkel out of the bag and shoved it in the suspect's face. "In the back of your closet I found *this*, still wet!"

At that the suspect toppled off the chair onto the floor.

"Another mystery bites the dust," said Garfield. "Sherlock Holmes, eat your heart out."

Just then Garfield heard the front door open. "I'm home," called Jon. Odie barked a greeting. "Hello, Odie," said Jon. "Hello, Bubbles." There was a pause. "Bubbles? Where are you?" said Jon. "GARFIELD!"

Jon stomped into the room. "Garfield, what happened to my fish?"

"Jon, I'm afraid Bubbles is Snack City," replied Garfield. "And there's the culprit." He pointed to the suspect, still lying on the floor.

"Pooky?!" cried Jon. "You expect me to believe that your teddy bear ate my goldfish? Garfield, how dumb do you think I am?"

"Tough question," replied Garfield. "And one that I've thought long and hard about."

"Just tell me, how do you explain that scuba mask and snorkel?"

"The latest fashion craze?" asked Garfield.

"No TV for a month!" shouted Jon, turning and stomping away.

Garfield bent down and scooped up Pooky. "Congratulations, old pal," said Garfield. "Looks like you're off the hook."

He gave the teddy bear a reassuring hug. "And now, how about some pizza?" He smiled slyly. "After all, a cat doesn't live by goldfish alone."